ROSIE saves the WORLD

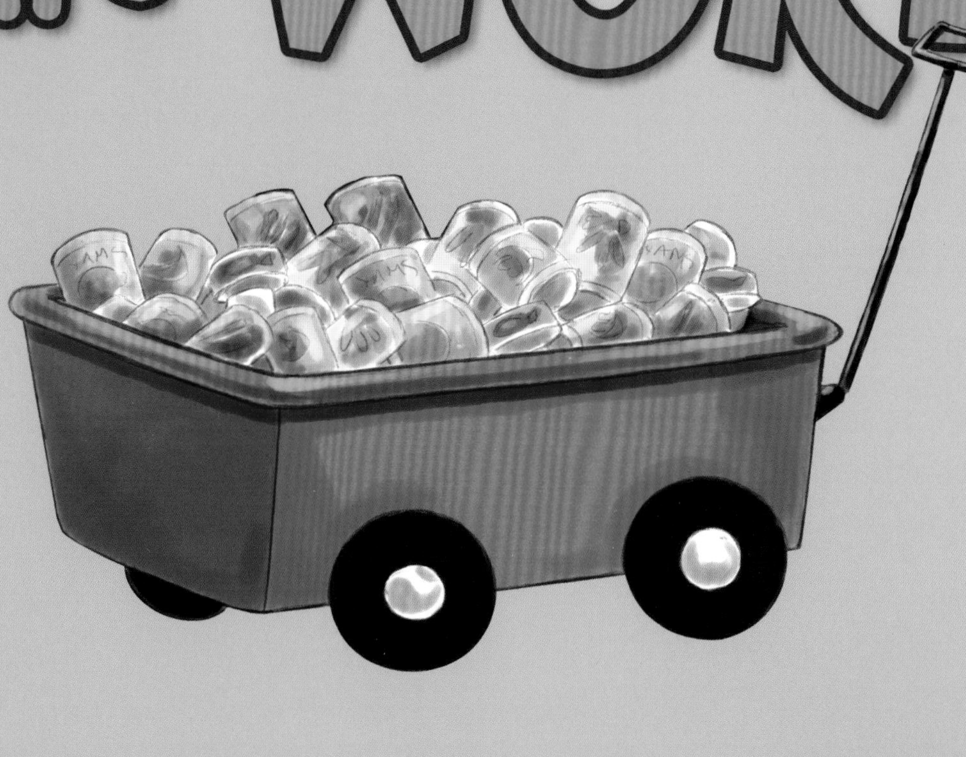

For my mother, Charlotte Herman—
My Superhero! —D.H.

For Linda, who makes the world a
kinder and friendlier place every day.
Thanks for all you do. —T.L.

KAR-BEN PUBLISHING
A division of Lerner Publishing Group, Inc.
241 First Avenue North
Minneapolis, MN 55401 USA
1-800-4-KARBEN

Website address: www.karben.com

Main body text set in Avenir LT Std 55 Roman 15/20.
Typeface provided by Adobe Systems.

Library of Congress Cataloging-in-Publication Data

Names: Herman, Debbie, author. | Lyon, Tammie, illustrator.
Title: Rosie saves the world / by Debbie Herman ; illustrated by Tammie Lyon.
Description: Minneapolis : Kar-Ben Publishing, [2017] | Summary: When Rosie learns about tikkun olam in Hebrew class she sets out to save the world, but then realizes she is neglecting important responsibilities at home. Includes facts about Areyvut.
Identifiers: LCCN 2016028086| ISBN 9781512420852 (lb : alk. paper) | ISBN 9781512420869 (pb : alk. paper)
Subjects: | CYAC: Voluntarism—Fiction. | Commandments (Judaism)— Fiction. | Jews—United States—Fiction.
Classification: LCC PZ7.1.H4936 Ros 2017 | DDC [E]—dc23

LC record available at https://lccn.loc.gov/2016028086

Manufactured in the United States of America
1-41256-23231-12/13/2016

ROSIE saves the WORLD

Debbie Herman

Illustrations by Tammie Lyon

KAR-BEN
PUBLISHING

Rosie was excited.

She was going to save the world!

Her Hebrew school class had been learning about *tikkun olam*, repairing the world by doing good deeds (her teacher called them *mitzvot*). Rosie was sure she could do good deeds—great deeds, in fact. So she set out to help the people in her neighborhood.

Rosie dusted off her old wagon. She was pulling it down the sidewalk when her mom came home.

"Rosie, honey, can you give me a hand with the groceries?
There are more in the car."

"I'd love to, Mom," said Rosie. "But I have to go save the
world! It's time for *Operation Can Collection!*"

Rosie knew it was a mitzvah to feed the hungry, so she knocked on the doors of neighbors she knew and asked them to donate cans of food.

They gave her tuna,

yams, baby carrots,

and asparagus.

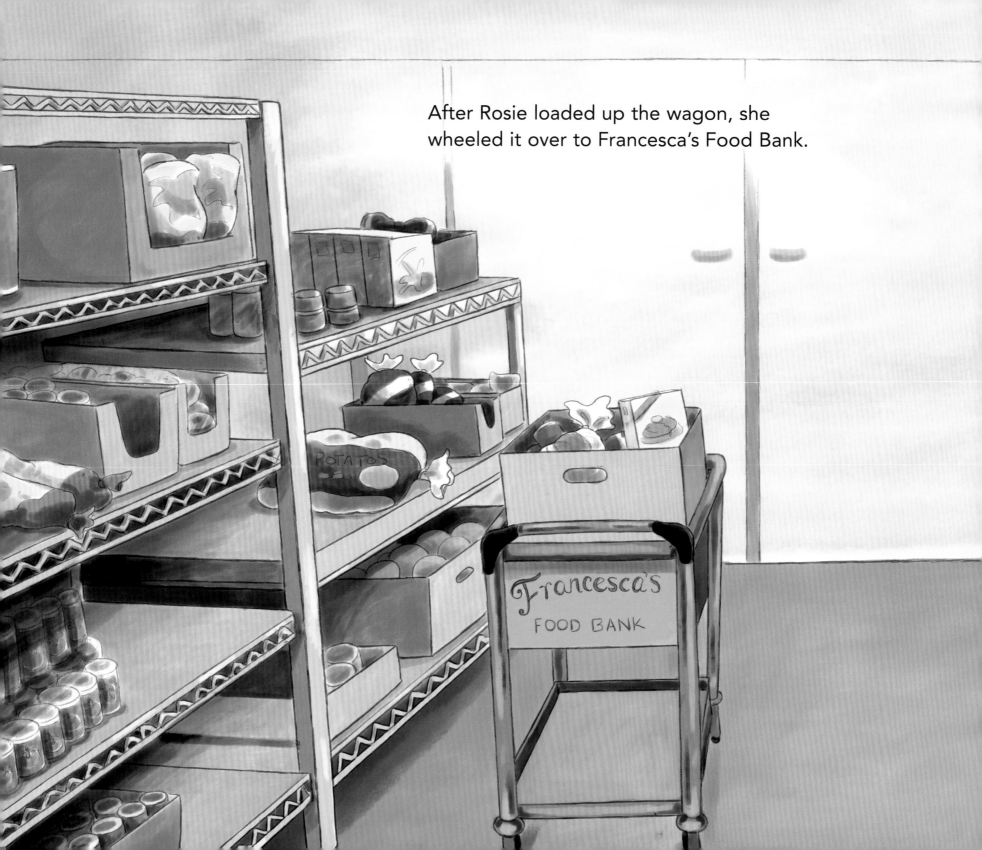

After Rosie loaded up the wagon, she wheeled it over to Francesca's Food Bank.

"How thoughtful!" exclaimed Francesca, looking at the collection of canned goods. "And just when our stock was running low. You're quite a superhero!"

Rosie smiled proudly. She could get used to this *tikkun* thing.

Rosie's next project was *Operation Tutor Tots*. She had learned it
was a mitzvah to teach others, so she decided to go to the library
to help little kids with their homework. As Rosie gathered her
tutoring supplies, her brother Simon called to her.

"Rosie, can you help me draw the letter *alef?* I keep messing up."

"Sorry, Sy," said Rosie. "Can't keep the tots waiting!"
And she ran out the door.

Later that week, Rosie got ready for *Operation Sing With Seniors*. She'd get to do the mitzvah of honoring the elderly while showcasing her musical talents. As Rosie tuned her ukulele, her dad walked into the room. "Hey, Rosie Cheeks!" he said. "How about coming with me to visit Grandma?"

"Next time," said Rosie. "Today I'm busy saving the world. But please give Grandma a kiss for me."

Rosie skipped over to the assisted living center, where she played her ukulele and sang. She even took requests. Afterward, she walked around and talked with the residents. They told her she was a star!

The next day, Rosie was in her room, creating a Save-the-World spreadsheet.

Her mom called to her, "Rosie, can you please clean out Leo's litter box? It's really starting to smell."

"I'll do it later, Mom," Rosie called back. "I'm busy planning new Save-the-World projects. And you just gave me an idea . . ."

Rosie added *Operation Pamper Pets* to her spreadsheet. She thought about how much fun it would be to help out at the animal shelter. After all, she knew it was a mitzvah to be kind to animals.

WAAAHHHH

On the way home from the animal shelter, Rosie heard crying coming from the Albert house. She knocked on the door to make sure everything was OK.

An exhausted-looking Mrs. Albert opened the door, bouncing her baby, Luis, in her arms. "I just can't get him to sleep," she explained, "And I have a deadline to meet for work . . ."

"Say no more!" said Rosie, scooping up baby Luis in her arms.

Rosie rocked Luis,

gave him a bottle,

and even changed his diaper.

When Luis was finally asleep, Rosie tidied up the living room.
And Mrs. Albert finished her work just in the nick of time.

"You're a life saver!" exclaimed Mrs. Albert, giving Rosie a big hug.
"I bet you're a huge help at home, aren't you?"

Rosie thought for a moment.

She thought of her mother and the grocery bags.

She thought of Simon trying to write an *alef.*

She thought of her father visiting Grandma without her.

And she thought of Leo in his stinky litter box.

"Well, actually . . ." Rosie stammered. "I . . . I have to go!"

And she raced out the door.

"Hiya, Sy!" said Rosie, plopping down next to her brother, who was on the sidewalk in front of their house. "Want some help with your chalk drawing?"

"Sure!" said Simon.

When they finished drawing the biggest dragon ever, Rosie helped Simon draw the letter *alef*.

Then Rosie went inside and cleaned out Leo's litter box. "Sorry about that," she told Leo, petting him. "It won't happen again."

Next she called her grandma. "How are you, Grandma?" asked Rosie. "It's been a while since we talked."

Finally, Rosie went to look for her mother. She found her in the pantry, dusting her cookie jar collection.

"Want some help?" asked Rosie.

"I'd love it," said her mother. "But I thought you were busy saving the world."

"I am," said Rosie, picking up a dust cloth. "By doing my best mitzvah project yet. **Operation Family Comes First!**"

Rosie took the superhero cookie jar and got to work. "I can save the rest of the world tomorrow."

About Areyvut

We live in a big, busy world. We see disasters far away—and help immediately. We see celebrations all over the Earth—and share in the rejoicing. The Jewish value of *tikkun olam* encourages us to try to repair the world. But while we focus on repairing the whole world, we also must not lose sight of our own family and our Jewish community. This is the important Jewish concept of Areyvut, which comes from the Hebrew phrase *Kol Yisrael arayvim zeh ba'zeh*: All Jews are responsible for one another.

Rosie is a girl with a heart big enough to embrace the world. She is a heroine, extending a helping hand to everyone. But, as Jewish values teach, and as Rosie learns, it is not enough to fix the entire world if we forget our responsibilities at home.

About the Author

Debbie Herman is a writer and editor, living in Jerusalem. She is the author of several books for children, including *Carla's Sandwich* and *From Pie Town to Yum Yum*. She hopes to save the world one book at a time.

About the Illustrator

Tammie Lyon is the award-winning author and illustrator of many books for children. Her previous books include the Eloise series as well as Katie Woo and the Pedro series. She lives in Cincinnati, Ohio with her husband, and loves spending the day in her studio with her dogs, Gus and Dudley.